Sister Magic

Violet Makes a Splash

BY **ANNE MAZER**

ILLUSTRATED BY BILL BROWN

SCHOLASTIC INC.

New York Toronto London Auckland Sydney
Mexico City New Delhi Hong Kong Buenos Aires

For Ellen Potter and Megan Shull

No part of this publication may be reproduced, stored in a retrieval system, or transmitted in any form or by any means, electronic, mechanical, photocopying, recording, or otherwise, without written permission of the publisher. For information regarding permission, write to
Scholastic Inc.
Attention: Permissions Department,
557 Broadway, New York, NY 10012.

ISBN-13: 978-0-439-87247-8
ISBN-10: 0-439-87247-2

Text copyright © 2007 by Anne Mazer.
Illustrations copyright © 2007 by Scholastic Inc.
SCHOLASTIC, LITTLE APPLE, SISTER MAGIC, and associated logos are trademarks and/or registered trademarks of Scholastic Inc.

12 11 10 9 8 7 6 5 4 3 2 1   7 8 9 10 11 12/0
                                                                40

Printed in the U.S.A.
First printing, July 2007

Chapter One

"We have serious work to do here, Violet," Mabel said. She scratched a mosquito bite on her arm, then picked up a pen.

"Okay, Mabel," said her little sister.

In the living room, clothes and appliances spilled out of boxes and bags. The girls were getting ready for the annual garage sale.

At the end of every summer, the entire neighborhood banded together to hold a giant garage sale. There were fourteen families. Everyone had a table.

Afterward, they had a party. There was delicious food and a pie-baking contest.

While the grown-ups ate, the neighborhood kids played games in the street.

It was one of Mabel's favorite nights of the year.

This year, Mabel was in charge of her family's garage sale table. She was ready.

She glanced at her list. "Today we have to sort through old clothes, winter boots, kitchen utensils, baby toys, books, and other items."

It was a big job, but Mabel could do it.

"Here's the plan. You hand me clothes," Mabel instructed her sister. "I fold and price them. Okay?"

"Okay," Violet agreed. She brought over a couple of baby sweaters. Then she wandered away.

"What are you doing, Violet?"

"Nothing." Violet pulled out a battered cape and ran her fingers over the purple fabric. "I like this," she said.

"It's a piece of old junk," Mabel said.

"No, it isn't." Violet draped the cape over her shoulders and studied her reflection in the mirror.

Mabel folded a little striped sweater and slapped a price tag on it. Then she folded a pale yellow one. "I'm done with the baby sweaters, Violet. Bring me something else to price."

But Violet wasn't listening.

"Violet?" Mabel frowned. "We're not going to get any work done like this."

Her little sister pranced and twirled around the living room. The purple cape billowed out behind her. She hummed a tune.

"Oh, never mind. I'll do it myself," Mabel grumbled.

Yesterday Mabel had said Violet could be her assistant. Now she wished that she had never made the offer.

She wished she had told Violet to find a play date instead.

Five-year-old Violet was nothing but trouble.

She was mischievous and quirky, and she always insisted on having her own way.

She didn't follow instructions; she wasn't reliable. Her face was always smudged. Her hair was always wild. Her clothes never matched.

Mabel, on the other hand, wore coordinated outfits, even in the summer. Her hair was always combed. Her face was always washed.

She was neat, organized, trustworthy, and helpful. She was eight years old and mature beyond her age.

Her mother thought that organizing a garage sale was too much work for an eight- and a five-year-old.

She was probably right about the five year old. But Mabel knew she could do it. With or without Violet.

She would show everyone. Mabel was going to have the best garage sale, *ever*.

Before she started work, Mabel made a list of things to do:

1. Sort books by title and subject.
2. Fold used clothing in piles according to color and size.
3. Hang up skirts, dresses, and coats.
4. Organize baby toys in bins.
5. Separate children's clothing into categories: "infant," "toddler," and "young child."
6. Price everything with color coded tags.

Mabel loved being in charge and running the show.

She loved doing things well.

She loved having people say, "I knew I could count on you, Mabel."

*   *   *

As Mabel worked, Violet climbed onto the couch and jumped off. The purple cape flew out behind her. Then she climbed back up and jumped again.

Mabel was still pricing when she heard the crash. She dropped everything and ran to her sister.

Violet had tripped over a box of wire hangers, banged into a small lamp, and fallen in the middle of some shopping bags.

"Are you all right?" Mabel cried.

Violet nodded. Things were scattered all around her. Her cape was twisted and torn. A hanger was caught on her foot.

She stood up slowly and brushed herself off.

"This is more of a mess than ever." Mabel tried to be patient. "If you're not going to help, could you at least stay out of the way?"

"Sorry, Mabel."

Mabel picked up a pair of lime green tights with only a tiny hole in the toe and wrote a price tag for them.

Violet climbed onto the couch again. "Watch me fly!"

"Did you hear what I just said?" Mabel felt exasperated. How many times did she have to repeat herself? "Stay out of my way! I'm busy!"

It was hopeless, she thought. Why had she ever thought of asking Violet to help? Violet made everything a hundred times more difficult.

A wind gusted across the room. Where was her troublemaking little sister now?

Then Mabel heard a giggle. It came from right above her head.

She looked up.

Violet was floating near the ceiling.

The purple cape swayed lightly in the breeze. Wire hangers hung from Violet's

arms like bracelets. Violet's feet dangled above Mabel's nose.

Mabel's heart began to pound. Her sister could do *this*? She could *fly*?

Chapter Two

There was magic in their family and Violet had it.

If you asked Mabel, this was a terrible mistake. It wasn't sensible, fair, or logical. She should have gotten the magic.

Mabel was the older sister. She followed rules and kept promises. She was careful, considerate, and responsible.

Violet was none of the above.

Besides, how could a five year old handle magic? Mabel wondered. Violet didn't even know her alphabet!

But she had the magic. And now, it seemed, she could fly.

"Come down, Violet!" Mabel begged.

"Please!" She really didn't need this right now.

Hovering near the ceiling, Violet peered into the light fixture. "Lots of dead bugs in here."

Mabel climbed onto the couch and tried to grab Violet's ankles. But her little sister wiggled out of her reach.

"I'll let you have my dessert tonight," Mabel cajoled. "I'll even buy you ice cream tomorrow."

Violet ignored her. She curled up in mid-air and turned upside down.

The purple cape fell over her head. Wire hangers dropped to the floor. Violet's skinny legs wobbled.

She suddenly plummeted downward, headfirst toward the floor.

Mabel jumped off the couch and ran to catch her sister. But she wasn't fast enough. *"Violet!"*

Luckily, Violet put out her hands and stopped just inches from the floor.

"Ta da!" she cried, flopping over onto her side.

Mabel's heart beat wildly. "What do you think you're doing, Violet? Are you crazy?"

"You told me to stay out of your way."

"I didn't tell you to *fly*," Mabel protested.

Violet stretched her arms and wriggled her toes. "What's wrong with flying?"

"It's dangerous, silly! You almost smashed yourself up!"

"But I didn't," Violet said smugly. "And besides, people fly in airplanes all the time."

"That's different," Mabel said. "That's science, and engineering, and, um, tickets. People don't fly by themselves."

"*I* do," Violet said with irritating logic.

Mabel took a deep breath. "Do you know why you can fly?"

"Because I'm going into kindergarten?"

Mabel rolled her eyes. Then she ordered herself to stay calm and mature.

She had to guide and advise her ignorant

little sister. Violet needed her advice. It wouldn't be easy, but Mabel could help her.

"What do you know about magic, Violet?"

"It's in fairy tales."

"It's real, too," Mabel explained. She felt a pang as she said it. Hadn't she promised her mother never to breathe a word of this to Violet?

She had promised never to speak of magic to *anyone*.

The magic came from her mother's side. Her mother hated it so much that she would barely admit it was real. Mabel's father didn't know about it. Mabel had only stumbled upon the truth by accident.

Mabel hated having secrets, especially from her family. But her mother had sworn her to secrecy.

And a promise was a promise. Mabel always kept promises, even if she didn't like them.

Just this once, though, she was going to bend the rules. Violet deserved to know what was going on.

Mabel had to protect her little sister.

So she took a deep breath and spoke the words. "You have magic, Violet."

Chapter Three

Violet didn't seem shocked or surprised that she had magic. "Oh," she said.

"That's it?" Mabel said. "Don't you want to ask me about it?"

Violet shrugged.

If Violet didn't have any questions, Mabel sure did.

"Did someone teach you to fly? Did you learn from a book?" she asked. "Did you practice in a dream?"

"Flying isn't hard," Violet said with a shrug. "Anyone can do it."

"Anyone with magic, you mean."

"*Anyone,*" Violet insisted.

"Not me. I can't fly. Most people can't." Mabel flapped her arms. "See?"

"That's not the way," Violet scolded. She got to her feet. "I'll show you, Mabel."

Violet leaned back, opened her arms, and floated a few feet in the air.

Then she came back down again. "See? It's simple. Now you try it."

If *she* had magic, Mabel wondered, would she share it with Violet?

She had to admit that the answer was no. She'd be telling Violet to keep her grubby hands off her powers.

It was nice of Violet to offer to help.

Because suddenly Mabel wanted more than anything to fly.

Mabel hoped that Violet was right. Maybe magic was more ordinary than anyone knew. Maybe both sisters had the magic gene. Hers just hadn't shown up yet.

If Mabel followed Violet's instruction,

she, too, would fly. Hadn't she flown in her dreams?

She arched her back, flung out her arms, and lost her balance. Just in time, she righted herself again.

What was she thinking?

"Don't go telling people they can fly," Mabel sputtered, "when they can't!" She scooped up a bunch of baby toys and dumped them in a bin.

Violet wrapped her cape around herself.

"What are you doing now?" Mabel demanded.

"Pretending," Violet said. She unwrapped the cape. "I'm a flower. I'm blooming."

"You're a violet," Mabel said. "Ha, ha, ha." She was going to have to have a sense of humor about this. As long as Violet didn't enchant herself into an actual flower, they were fine.

Mabel leaned over to pick up a rattle. When she looked up, Violet was in the air again.

Her little sister was like yeast. She kept rising.

"Come back down here!" Mabel ordered.

Violet turned upside down and began to walk on the ceiling.

"You're leaving footprints, Violet! Wipe them off!" Mabel called.

Violet took the corner of her T-shirt and dusted the ceiling with it. Then she floated back down.

Mabel was waiting for her. "You just

can't fly around the house or leave foot-prints on the ceiling," she informed her.

She hoped Violet would listen. "You can't let anyone know that you have magic."

"Why not?"

"Mom and Dad will be so unhappy if they find out," Mabel said in a low voice. "You don't want to make them unhappy, do you?"

Violet bit her lip. "No," she said.

"We have to be normal." Mabel had an uneasy feeling as she said these words. "Or we have to pretend to be."

"I like pretending," Violet said.

"This is a different kind of pretending," Mabel said. "Do you understand?"

"Yes, Mabel," Violet said. She waved a hand dreamily in the air. A couple of chocolate bars dropped into her pocket.

Violet handed one to Mabel. It was white chocolate, Mabel's favorite.

She stared at it for a moment, then she broke off a small piece. It was delicious.

"How did you do that?" Mabel whispered.

Violet only shrugged. She wiped her hands on the side of her already dirty T-shirt and bit into a milk chocolate bar.

Mabel wondered what else Violet could do. Could she change tap water into soda, like a character did in one of Mabel's favorite books?

Could she conjure up cones of cotton candy? Change the hair color on Mabel's dolls? Create beads for Mabel's handmade jewelry? Could she make a bike go extra fast? Or a swing go extra high?

What if Mabel had a say in Violet's magic?

She'd tell Violet how to use it and, especially, how to keep it safe.

Violet could fly, but Mabel could explain
the rules.

Her sister had the magic; she had the
brains.

It was a perfect combination.

Chapter Four

Mabel picked up one of her father's old shirts. They hadn't gotten much done. Violet's magic was a full-time job in itself.

"I'm done playing," Violet announced. "I want to help."

"Finally," Mabel said. "See these stuffed animals? They're everywhere. Put them all together and throw them in that box."

"Okay, Mabel." Violet laid her cape on the floor and piled the toys on it. Then she tied it up like a giant handkerchief and emptied everything into the box.

Trust Violet not to do things the ordinary way.

Mabel couldn't complain, though. At least her little sister was helping out.

"Shall I mark this for two dollars or three?" Mabel pointed to an old alarm clock. "What do you think, Violet?"

"Thirty-three thousand dollars," Violet said. "And twenty-twelve cents."

"Thanks," Mabel said. "You're a big help."

"I am," Violet agreed.

Mabel congratulated herself. Violet had listened and understood. She now knew that she had to be careful how and where she used her magic.

It was because Mabel had explained everything so well.

Then their mother walked in.

"You girls haven't done much yet," she said in surprise. "You're usually so organized, Mabel."

"Violet and I have been, um, talking," Mabel said.

"That's okay, honey," her mother said. "No big deal."

She touched a faded sweater. "I wore this sweater on my first date with your father. It's older than you and Violet."

Mabel tried to think of the time before she was born. It gave her an odd feeling to imagine her parents without her.

Her mother glanced over at Violet. "Are you Mabel's big helper?"

"I'm a superhero." Violet looped the cape over her shoulders and ran around the room. "Watch me fly!"

Mabel gasped. Hadn't her little sister understood anything?

"*No*, Violet!" Mabel lurched forward to stop her sister.

"Hey, leave me alone!"

"Mabel?" her mother said. "Chill out."

Mabel blushed. She dropped her sister's arm. She pointed to the overflowing bags and boxes and mumbled about all the work they had left to do.

"Don't get carried away," her mother said. "It's just a garage sale. If you feel overwhelmed, I'll pitch in."

"No, Mom, I can do it myself, " Mabel said quickly.

It wasn't just her pride. She was really nervous about what Violet might do.

If Mabel didn't watch out, her sister's magic might unleash a family disaster.

But could she keep track of Violet every single second?

"I bet you need inspiration," her mother said. "Well, Dad and I have decided to take everyone on a weekend trip with the money we earn. Any ideas?"

"Wet Water!" Mabel and Violet cried at the same time.

"The water adventure park?" their mother said. "Sounds like a plan."

"We better get cracking," Mabel said to Violet. "We want to go to Wet Water, don't we?"

Her little sister snapped her fingers.

"That won't help," Mabel said. She kneeled down to pick up a pair of slippers, then glanced at her sister. "Why don't you hand me a —"

Her jaw dropped open.

In the blink of an eye, the bags and boxes overflowing with junk had vanished.

Everything was folded, sorted, stacked, and shelved. The garage sale was completely organized.

"Violet?" Mabel whispered. She was having trouble breathing. "Did *you* do that?"

"Yes," Violet said.

"How —" Mabel started to say. Violet was a slob. How had she done it? Even with magic, it was stunning how neat everything was.

Just then their mother came back into the room.

She stared, speechless, at the orderly piles. "That was fast," she finally said.

"Uh, we really want to go to the water park," Mabel mumbled.

"I guess you do," her mother agreed. She picked up an empty box. "Keep up the good work, girls."

"Sure, Mom."

Mabel waited until her mother was gone. Then she turned to Violet.

"I'm a helper," Violet said.

"You sure are." She patted her little sister on the back. "Great job, Violet."

A slow smile spread over Mabel's face. Maybe magic wasn't so bad after all.

Chapter Five

"I still can't get over what you two did for the garage sale," their mother raved at dinner.

It was just the three of them. Their mother had defrosted lima beans, corn, peas, and burgers for a quick supper.

"It was nothing," Mabel said modestly. She pushed her lima beans to the other side of the plate.

All Mabel had done was put price stickers on everything. For some reason, Violet's magic didn't include pricing.

"I know you're organized, Mabel, but this is beyond my wildest expectations," her mother continued. "And Violet! You're wonderful!"

For once Mabel had to agree. She grabbed Violet's hand and held it up in the air.

"We have sister power," she said.

"We have sister magic!" Violet said.

Mabel glanced anxiously at her mother. Fortunately, her mother's mind seemed to be elsewhere.

"You girls look so cute together," she said. "Don't move. I'm going to get the

camera. I'll be right back." She rushed from the room.

"Careful!" Mabel reminded Violet. "We don't want to upset Mom."

"It was just a joke," Violet protested.

"You can't even say that word —" Mabel broke off as her mother returned.

"Ready?" their mother said. She held up a digital camera. "Smile!"

Mabel glanced at Violet. Her little sister had a mischievous look on her face. It made Mabel very nervous.

Violet pointed her little finger at the lima beans on the table. She hated lima beans.

Uh oh. . . .

"Violet, do you want to play ponies with me after supper?" Mabel said quickly. "We can play in my room."

Violet's eyes widened. Her hand fell to her side.

Mabel kept her ponies hidden on a high shelf in her closet inside a locked box. The ponies were very special. She never let her little sister touch them.

"Mabel, what a good big sister you are," her mother said.

Usually, Mabel loved praise. But today she felt uncomfortable.

She was just making sure that lima beans didn't turn into jumping beans, or jelly beans, or key lime pie.

"Now?" Violet demanded. "We can play ponies now?"

"Are you finished eating?" Mabel asked.

Her little sister pushed away the lima beans. Then she smiled.

The camera flashed. "Perfect," her mother said.

Chapter Six

"You have to wash your hands, face, and feet before you come into my room," Mabel ordered.

"My feet, too?" Violet protested.

"I saw those footprints you left on the ceiling!"

While Violet was washing up, Mabel went into her closet. She found the hidden place where she kept her ponies. She took down the box and unlocked it.

There were twelve ponies.

She set them up in a circle. She brushed their manes. She touched their smooth, glossy coats.

They were all different. She loved
them all.

The door opened. Violet came in.

"Sit down here, Violet." Mabel patted
the carpet next to her. "You can look but
don't touch."

Violet sat cross-legged on the floor. She
stared intently at the ponies.

It was very quiet in the room. A breeze
came through the window. It ruffled the
ponies' tails.

One of the ponies twitched its head.
Then another snorted. One pawed the
ground.

Mabel looked
over at her little
sister. "Violet?"
she said. "Is that
you?"

Violet didn't
answer. She was
deep in thought.

One by one, the ponies began to move. They pranced, galloped in a circle, and then began to race.

Mabel had never played ponies like this before.

It was marvelous. It was miraculous. It was magic.

The ponies headed for the door.

"No!" Mabel cried in panic. She rushed to the door and slammed it shut just in time.

Mabel stood with her back against the door and watched the ponies run wild in her bedroom.

They made their way onto Mabel's desk, knocking over her pictures and lamp. They climbed onto the bed. They hid under the pillows and pawed at her covers.

Then they ran toward an open window.

"Stop them, Violet!" Mabel begged. "Before they escape!"

Violet snapped her fingers. The ponies slowed, then stopped.

Quickly, before any more magic could

start, Mabel gathered them up and locked them away.

She straightened her desk and picked up the lamp.

"Can we do it again?" Violet asked.

Mabel didn't answer for a moment. Then slowly she nodded her head yes.

Chapter Seven

It was the hottest day of the summer.

Mabel, her friend Simone, and Violet were in a small inflatable pool in the backyard. They were trying to stay cool.

Simone had long black hair that she wore in a braid around her head.

She had a wide smile and crooked teeth. She wore pointy blue glasses everywhere, even in the pool.

"Because I can't see without them," Simone said.

"Try squinting your eyes," Mabel suggested.

Simone took off the glasses and squinted.

"It doesn't help," she said, putting them back on her face.

Mabel splashed water on her face and arms.

"Are you excited about the garage sale?" Simone asked. "I can't wait!"

"I'm too hot to think about it," Mabel said in a cranky voice.

Next to her, Violet was pouring buckets of water over her own head.

"Aren't you sick of doing that?" Mabel asked. "I'm sick of watching it."

"Aw, she's cute," Simone said.

"Sometimes," Mabel admitted. Everything was getting on her nerves today. "Don't you wish this pool was bigger? Then we could really cool off."

"The pool is fine," Simone reassured her. "We're having fun. Right, Violet?"

"Right," said Violet. Water streamed over her face as she emptied the bucket on her head once again.

Mabel sighed. She wished Violet was more mature. But Simone didn't seem to mind.

Simone picked up a beach ball. "Let's play catch!" she said. She threw the ball to Violet, who caught it and tossed it back.

"Now it's your turn, Mabel," Simone said.

In a minute, all three were throwing the ball back and forth. Violet forgot about the bucket. Mabel forgot about her worries.

"I haven't had this much fun in a long

time," Mabel said when they stopped to catch their breath.

"Me, either," Simone said. Her glasses were crooked. Strands of dripping hair hung in her face.

Violet adjusted her floaty around her waist. It was a white cat with pointed ears. "I'm going to swim," she announced. "Everyone watch."

She paddled for a few yards. Then she stopped. "Wasn't that good?"

"Yes," Mabel said, frowning. Something was wrong here. She couldn't figure it out.

"Wait for me, Violet." Simone set her glasses on the grass and plunged into the water.

Then suddenly she stopped. "What's different?" she said with a puzzled expression.

"I don't know," Mabel said. "Probably nothing."

She looked at Simone. She looked at her

little sister. She looked at the white cat floaty. It seemed to wink at her.

Then she looked at the pool.

Aha! That was it. The pool was bigger now.

The small inflatable pool was now a much larger inflatable pool.

Mabel knew where this new pool had come from, and it wasn't the big box store on the highway.

It had to be Violet's magic again.

Chapter Eight

"Where did you get the pool?" Simone asked. "It's really great."

"My mother got it on sale," Mabel said, thinking quickly. "You know, those end-of-season clearance bargains."

Simone smiled. "My mother likes those, too. Are you going to sell the old one at the garage sale?"

"Maybe." Mabel ducked under water. "Race you to the edge," she said.

She had to keep Simone busy. She didn't want her thinking too much.

When Simone had gone home, Mabel took Violet aside.

"This pool is lots of fun," she said slowly. She wished she didn't have to say what she said next. "But it has to go."

"No!" Violet said.

"It's one thing to play ponies in my room," Mabel said. "But it's another to go changing swimming pools right under Simone's feet. Lucky she didn't ask too many questions. Understand?"

"Yes, Mabel."

"Can you fix it?"

Violet slowly nodded.

"When I come back out, this pool better be gone." Mabel went upstairs to change into dry clothes.

Mabel changed out of her swim suit and sat down at her desk to think. There was a lot to think about.

What if Simone asked more questions? What if her mother saw the pool? What if a neighbor came by?

What would happen if Violet's magic was discovered?

Mabel took out paper and pen and began to make a list.

She wrote at the top of the sheet of paper: "Things that could happen if my parents find out about Violet's magic."

1. Mother devastated.
2. Father shocked.
3. Father and mother angry at me for keeping secrets.
4. Father angry at mother for keeping secrets.
5. Parents divorce?

That was such a terrible thought, Mabel ripped up the list and started again.

"Things that could happen if neighbors find out about Violet's magic."

1. Neighbors think our family is strange.
2. They call us "those magic people"

and won't let their kids play
with us.

3. Doors slam when we walk down the
street. No one will ride bikes or ice
skate with us.

Mabel ripped that one up, too. "More Things," she wrote on a fresh sheet of paper. "Things that could happen when Violet and I go back to school."

1. Violet gets placed in a special class
for kids with magic — by herself.
2. No one will shop at my father's
clothing store. They're afraid that
the gym shorts are enchanted.
3. His store goes out of business.
4. Parents pull us out of school and
tutor us at home (if they're not
divorced).

Mabel frowned and started another list.

"Really Terrible Things," she wrote.
"Things that could happen if the whole world found out."

1. Television reporters camp out on our front lawn.
2. We can't leave the house.
3. Scientists find out about Violet and want to do experiments.
4. They whisk her away to their laboratories.
5. They force Violet to drink strange

medicines and to fly at all hours of the night.

6. They keep the rest of the family in cells to observe us, too.

"Conclusions." Mabel wrote. This was supposed to be the good part, where she settled everything in her mind and made decisions. "Results of Violet's magic, if discovered."

1. Mom's life ruined.
2. Dad's life ruined.
3. My life ruined.
4. Violet's life ruined.

Mabel laid down her pen. She tore all the lists into tiny little pieces. Then she went to the window to see if Violet had followed her instructions.

It was time to get serious about Violet's magic. She had to keep it under wraps. This time, for real.

Chapter Nine

The pool was still there.

Violet sat cross-legged in front of it. She appeared to be meditating. Had she even tried to get rid of it?

Mabel leaned her head out of the window. "Listen, Violet," she began. Then she stopped as, right in front of her eyes, the big inflatable pool vanished.

So Violet was listening, after all. Mabel blew her a kiss. "You're the best —" she began to say.

Then another pool appeared. It wasn't the little inflatable pool. It was a full-size, aboveground swimming pool.

A deck appeared, then a wooden safety

fence. Chairs whizzed onto the deck, and water toys plunked into a bin.

Violet rubbed her hands together and a table with an umbrella appeared.

"Violet," Mabel gasped.

"Don't interrupt me, Mabel," she said. "Aren't I doing a good job?"

"You have to change it back. *Please!*"

"Why?" Violet asked. "I love it. You will, too."

Mabel lowered her voice. "What will Mom say? Or Dad?"

"They'll be happy. I know it."

The cat floaty winked. This time Mabel was sure of it.

"Violet!" Mabel didn't care who heard her. "Be sensible!"

Her little sister stuck out her tongue. Then she walked away.

Mabel rushed down to the backyard. She was going to make her sister change the pool back. But Violet was gone.

From below, the pool looked bigger and even more impressive.

Mabel went over to the safety fence. It was solid and real and smelled of fresh varnish. She unlocked the gate and climbed to the deck.

Violet had thought of everything: clear blue water, diving board, life jackets, and even pool cleaners.

How had a five year old done this?

And how could she refuse to undo it?

"Violet!" Mabel yelled.

There was no answer.

Mabel sank onto the nearest chair. She couldn't help noticing how comfortable it was.

Her little sister definitely had a talent.

And it was definitely out of control.

"Mabel!" It was her mother.

"Coming!" Mabel yelled. "Right away, Mom!"

She ran down the stairs and locked the gate behind her so that Violet couldn't wander in.

Even if she *could* conjure up pools, her little sister didn't know how to swim yet.

Chapter Ten

Her mother wanted her to post flyers for the garage sale around the neighborhood. She had just printed a stack from the computer.

"All right," Mabel agreed. "I'll ride my bike."

"Can I come, too?" It was Violet. She was wearing her cat floaty and a pair of red flippers.

"No way!" What if her little sister decided to turn her bicycle into a unicycle? Or a hang glider? Or a horse?

"Besides," Mabel added, "you can't ride a bike wearing a floaty and flippers."

"I can, too," Violet insisted.

"Why don't you help me bake, Violet?" her mother said. "I'm going to start the pies for the pie-baking contest. You can bake your very own pie. Maybe you'll win a prize."

Violet's face lit up. "I'll make a black-bird pie," she said. "Just like the nursery rhyme."

"How cute," her mother said.

"No, it isn't," Violet said.

Mabel shot her a warning look.

"It's my pie and I'll bake it the way I want," Violet said, sticking out her tongue.

"Of course you will, sweetheart," her mother said.

Mabel turned to leave, then stopped at the door. There were a lot of things she needed to say to Violet.

But since her mother was right there, Mabel said the only thing she could.

"While I'm gone, Mom, don't look into the backyard. Okay?"

"Didn't you girls clean up after yourselves?"

"Well, um, honestly, no," Mabel said. "And, you know, Violet and I want to clean up the backyard before you see it. Don't we, Violet, dear?"

"Of course not, Mabel, dear," Violet replied.

"I love the way you two are getting along lately," their mother said.

"Do you *promise*, Mom?" Mabel said again.

"Go post the flyers and don't worry," her mother said. "You worry too much, Mabel."

Ha! Mabel thought as she wheeled her bike out of the garage. If only her mother knew what she had to worry about!

She felt as if a ten-ton weight had landed on her shoulders. Was this what it was like to be a grown-up?

Two hours later, Mabel was home again. She leaned her bike against the garage wall and went inside.

"Mom? Violet?"

No one answered. It was quiet. Too quiet.

In the kitchen, pies were cooling on racks. They smelled delicious.

But her mother and Violet weren't there.

From the yard came the sounds of laughter and splashing.

Mabel ran to the back door and opened it quickly.

Chapter Eleven

"Mabel!" her mother cried. "Can you believe this pool?"

"Uh," Mabel said. She was in shock.

Her mother and little sister were floating in a new, Olympic-size, in-ground swimming pool.

"Where did it come from?" her mother asked. Fortunately, she didn't seem to expect an answer. "I can't figure out how he did this."

"*He?*" Mabel finally found her voice. Did her mother think that Uncle Vartan was responsible?

Her mother dove underwater and came

up for air. "He's so thoughtful! I'm one *very* lucky woman."

She didn't usually speak this way about her brother Vartan. The mere mention of his name made her eyes flash and her lips tighten.

He was the only other person with the family magic. Only she and Mabel knew about it.

Maybe Uncle Vartan had shown up while Mabel was posting flyers. Maybe he had come to save the secret and the day.

Mabel was only sorry she had missed him. She would have liked to have talked to him about Violet's magic.

And, of course, thanked him for the pool.

"It was really great of Uncle Vartan to give us a pool," she said.

"It wasn't Vartan," her mother said. "It was your father, of course."

"Oh," Mabel said. "I knew that."

Then the gate opened and Simone walked in.

✳   ✳   ✳

"Another bargain?" Simone frowned at Mabel. "This is the third pool I've seen in your yard today."

"Um," Mabel said. Actually, there had been four pools in their yard today. She hoped this was the last one.

"Your mother sure likes sales," Simone said suspiciously.

Mabel glanced in her mother's direction to see if she had heard. But she was swimming underwater again.

"Do you like our new pool, Simone?" Violet asked.

"It's great," Simone said. "How did it get here so fast?"

"That's just what I'd like to know," Mabel's mother said as she emerged, dripping. "I don't know how my husband did this."

Simone raised an eyebrow.

"Me, neither," Mabel agreed. "It's quite

a surprise." She looked meaningfully at Violet.

"It's practically magic," Simone said.

"It *is* magic," Violet piped up.

Mabel was having trouble breathing. She couldn't think; she couldn't speak.

But Simone only laughed. "Yeah, right, Violet. Like magic even exists."

Chapter Twelve

"What a day," Mabel's father said. "And now I've missed your mother, too. She rushed past me in the driveway."

"She was late for a meeting," Mabel said.

"That woman is always busy." He went to the refrigerator, took out a cold soda, and popped the tab. "I'm going to relax on the back porch. Want to join me?"

"Um, Dad?" Mabel said uncomfortably. She didn't want him in the backyard, unless the pool had vanished into the night. But somehow she didn't believe that it had.

"Can we stay inside?" she asked.

"Too many mosquitoes for you?" Her

father flipped on the porch light. "I'll light citronella candles."

He glanced out the window, then stared. He rubbed his eyes and blinked several times. "Do I see what I think I see?"

Mabel nodded.

"Is that why you didn't want to go out on the porch?"

Mabel nodded again. She didn't know what to say.

He opened the back door and gestured for her to follow him. Together they walked in silence to the pool.

The moon came out from behind a cloud and was reflected in the still, dark water.

"How did she do it?" he finally said. "It's magic."

"Magic?" Mabel repeated.

"Magic," her father said again. "When I look at this pool, I believe in it."

Relief welled up inside Mabel. He knew. She didn't know how, but he had figured it all out. She didn't even have to break her promise.

Her father was going to be there for her, like always. It would be so good to tell him the truth about Violet.

"Dad, I didn't want to say anything —"

"Of course not," he interrupted. "It would have spoiled the surprise."

"Oh, that," Mabel said. She was about to tell him just how many surprises Violet had sprung on her today, when he spoke again.

"It's amazing what she's done."

Mabel nodded in agreement. Not many five year olds could conjure up Olympic-size swimming pools. "But, Dad, we have to be careful."

"You're right," he said. "Violet can't swim, and then there are the neighbors. We don't want any accidents."

Mabel frowned. "That's the least of our problems."

"You're worrying about lawsuits? Leave

those problems to your mom and me. You just enjoy the pool, okay?"

Her father put his arm around her shoulder. "Tell me, Mabel. How did your mom do this? I didn't know she could keep a secret so well."

"Mom?" Mabel said in dismay.

Her father hadn't understood anything after all — except the part about her mother being good at keeping secrets. He had *that* right.

"It's just like her to surprise me. She's so thoughtful. I'm one lucky guy. I can't wait to thank her."

Haven't I heard this before? Mabel thought.

Chapter Thirteen

When Mabel went downstairs for breakfast the next morning, she was afraid.

Today's the garage sale, she thought, *and my parents will have figured out the truth about the pool.*

She hoped they wouldn't ask her the questions that she didn't want to answer.

Mabel approached the table slowly.

"You're the best," her father was saying.

"No, you are," her mother said.

Mabel tugged at her ears. *"Best?"* Had she heard correctly? Or had her father actually called her mother a "beast"?

Her father poured out coffee. "Cream?" he said. "Sugar for my honey?"

"Thank you," her mother answered. She took a sip of the coffee and looked deeply into his eyes. *"You're* the honey."

They gazed at each other like teenagers. They didn't even notice Mabel.

This wasn't what she had expected.

"You're so thoughtful," her father said to her mother. *"You* should take credit for what you did."

"The same to you, darling," her mother said. She blew her husband a kiss.

"Sandra!" her father said.

"Arthur!" her mother said.

"Whoa! Whoa!" Mabel said. She was starting to feel a little dizzy. She sat down and poured herself a glass of orange juice.

"Good morning! It's garage sale day," she said. "Do we have quarters for the cash box? Is the awning up? Did Dad get the folding chairs from the attic?"

Her parents were too absorbed in each other to answer.

"Mom? Dad?" Mabel wished she had a ruler to bang on the table. "Quit cooing and start acting like parents again! The garage sale is only an hour away. Help me get ready!"

"I'm ready for a dip in the pool," her father said. "Our beautiful, new, Olympic-size swimming pool."

"Me, too." Mabel's mother threw down her napkin.

Arm in arm, her parents went outside.

Would the cool water of the pool shock their brains, Mabel wondered. And if so, would that be good or bad?

They might stop mooning over each other. They might start thinking again. They might realize the truth about the pool.

If they did, someone had to make sure that things were explained properly.

Mabel gulped down her orange juice and ran after them.

This is all Violet's fault, she thought. *This is all happening because of her magic.*

As Mabel ran down the stairs toward the pool, her father was going back into the house.

"Forgot the towels," he said. "Can't swim without towels."

Mabel hurried toward her mother. Maybe she could say something to her now, while they were alone. At least her mother knew magic existed. At least she wouldn't have to explain *that*.

"Uh, Mom?" Mabel said.

Her mother was standing at the edge of the pool. She blinked at the bright sun. "What is it, Mabel?"

"I, uh —" Mabel began. "Um." She tried to think how to explain what had happened, but not a single phrase came to mind.

Her mother gasped.

Mabel looked up. Had Violet flown out her bedroom window in her pajamas? Was she tossing dirty laundry down on the lawn? Or turning somersaults on the roof?

But Violet was nowhere in sight. Mabel glanced at the pool.

Uncle Vartan was stretched out on a large rubber raft. He was fully clothed in a sky blue suit with blue leather shoes and silver socks. His leather briefcase was by his side.

It was Mabel's turn to gasp. How had Uncle Vartan known to show up *now*?

Swimming pool waves sloshed wildly, but never touched Uncle Vartan. Everything on the raft was perfectly dry.

It was magic.

Mabel stepped forward. But before she could say a word, Uncle Vartan smiled, waved briefly, and vanished into thin air.

Mabel's mother turned very pale.

And then Mabel's father was there with the towels. "Here you are, sweetie," he said to his wife, draping a towel over her shoulders. "I still can't get over this pool. Thank you so much."

Her mother didn't answer for a moment. Then she said, in a small voice, "You're welcome."

She glanced at Mabel. They looked at each other for a long moment. Then her mother dove into the pool.

✳   ✳   ✳

Back in her room, Mabel made a quick list.

Minuses

Mother knows the pool is magic.
She knows I know, too.
She lied to Dad.
She knows I know she lied.

Pluses

Mother knows the pool is magic.
She knows I know, too.
She lied to Dad.
She knows I know she lied.

Plus Pluses

She thinks Uncle Vartan did it.
She is letting Dad think that SHE did it.
Violet's magic still undiscovered.
Secret safe.

But barely. We must be careful.

Feeling relieved, Mabel hid the list in a desk drawer. Then she ran downstairs to get ready for the garage sale.

Chapter Fourteen

At 8:50 A.M. sharp, Mabel took her station behind the folding table.

Color-coded price stickers gleamed in the sunlight.

The neatly creased folds of the clothing seemed to say, "Good job, Mabel."

The cash box sat next to her like a trusted helper.

Mabel sat up straight in her chair. She had taken care of everything.

She had had a talk with Violet.

"No used books whizzing through the air," she said. "No clothes folding or unfolding themselves. *And absolutely no more swimming pools!*"

"Mom and Dad love the pool," Violet said.

"So?" Mabel said. "That doesn't mean anything. They love *you*, too."

Violet scowled at her.

"Because you're lovable," Mabel quickly added. "At least sometimes. Now promise me you'll stay away from magic today."

Violet didn't answer.

"Violet? Please? Please? *Please!*"

"Oh, okay," Violet finally said. She looked down at her feet. "Don't you like the pool, Mabel?" she asked in a small voice.

"Yes," she admitted. "I love it, Violet." She lowered her voice. "But four pools in one day is too much!"

"No more pools," Violet promised. "This one is enough."

"Thank goodness," Mabel said.

A car pulled up in front of the house and a man and a woman got out. They walked up the driveway to the table where Mabel sat.

"Are we late?" the woman asked. "Is all the good stuff gone already?"

The man began to paw through the neat, organized stacks of clothing.

He tossed sweaters and shirts in a heap. He unfolded pants. He put men's bathing suits on top of women's socks.

Mabel hated to see the mess.

"Will you accept a dollar for this?" he asked, holding up one of her father's sweaters.

"I'll take a dollar fifty," Mabel said.

"All right," he said, holding out a couple

of crumpled dollar bills. "You drive a hard bargain."

Mabel smiled proudly as she counted out his change. That was one dollar and fifty cents toward the water park admission.

His wife carried over a spatula, a lamp shade, and a doily. "I see you have a fancy new swimming pool."

"Must have cost a pretty penny," her husband added.

Mabel didn't answer.

"I bet you're really popular right now," the woman went on, digging cash out from a battered floral purse. "I bet everyone wants to be your friend."

"No," Mabel said. She hoped that it wasn't true.

She wanted everyone to love her for her coordinated outfits, her friendly smile, and her fairness at games, not for her pool.

Chapter Fifteen

The next customer was their nosy neighbor, Jeanne.

Her hair was in curlers. She was wearing a ratty blue bathrobe and bedroom slippers. She carried a straw purse embroidered with sunflowers.

She rummaged through the piles, tossing sweaters on top of pants and shoes into boxes of books.

Then she picked up an alarm clock. "Does this work?"

"Yes," Mabel said.

She dug her hands into her bathrobe pockets and plunked some quarters and dimes on the table. Then she pocketed the alarm clock.

"You have a new pool in your backyard." It sounded like an accusation.

"Um, yes, we do," Mabel said. Did people want to talk about anything else?

"I never heard a single sound," Jeanne said with a frown. "I never saw a single workman."

Mabel thought quickly. "We didn't want to disturb the neighbors."

"Who installed it?"

"It was, uh, a . . . surprise."

"I hope you don't have a lot of loud pool parties."

"Don't worry." Mabel decided to change the subject. "Are you coming to the party tonight?"

Jeanne didn't get a chance to answer. Violet crept up behind them. "Boo!" she yelled.

Jeanne jumped. Her straw purse fell to the ground. "Now that's not nice," she said, leaning over to pick it up. "It's not nice to scare people."

"Violet," Mabel said, "don't startle the neighbors."

Muttering to herself, Jeanne shuffled away.

"She's cranky," Violet said.

Mabel frowned at her little sister. "Get lost, Violet. "

"Why?" Violet picked up a frilly baby bib. "I want to help."

"I don't think so," Mabel said. "You've done more than enough already."

She glanced up. Cars were pulling up to

the curb. People were streaming toward the houses. "Look, it's getting busy."

Violet looked at the messy table. "I'll help you, Mabel."

Before Mabel could stop her, everything was neatly folded again.

"You promised," Mabel hissed. *"No magic!"*

Violet smiled. Then she skipped into the house.

Chapter Sixteen

"I've got everything under control," Mabel announced to her father an hour or two later.

He plunked down a glass of lemonade. "You've been working hard. I thought you might be thirsty."

"Thanks, Dad."

"Do you want to jump into the pool for a few minutes?" her father offered. "I can take your place here for fifteen minutes."

"Oh, no thanks," Mabel said. "I'll wait until the sale is over."

She opened the cash box and handed a stack of bills to her father. "Is this enough to take Violet and me to the water park?"

He counted up the cash. "We've got one hundred and sixty-two dollars here. That's more than enough."

"Hooray!" Mabel cried.

"But don't forget, we have our own water park now," he pointed out. "Thanks to your mother."

"Yeah," Mabel mumbled. "Mom is great."

It was true. Her mother *was* great. And so was the pool. If only she wasn't so nervous about people finding out where it had really come from!

If only she wasn't so worried about what magic Violet was going to do next!

Her father folded the bills and put them in an envelope. Then he glanced toward the street. "Here comes Jeanne."

"Again?" Mabel said in dismay.

Their nosy neighbor shuffled up the driveway. She took a handkerchief out of her bathrobe pocket and blew her nose loudly. "I wanted to ask, who did your pool?"

"You'll have to ask my wife," her father said before Mabel could stop him. "Honey!!!"

Her mother came out of the house.

"Who installed your pool?" Jeanne asked.

Oh no, Mabel thought. Her face got hot. Her stomach felt sick. She wondered if she was going to throw up.

Her mother laughed a little too loudly. "I, uh, forgot! You know what a terrible memory I have."

"You have a great memory, honey," her husband said, putting his arm around her shoulder.

"What about receipts?" Jeanne asked her. "You must have kept them."

"Sorry, I'm terribly disorganized," Mabel's mother said. "It would take me months to find them."

Jeanne turned to Mabel's father.

"Don't look at me," he said. "*I* didn't have anything to do with the pool."

"Do *you* remember?" Jeanne asked Mabel.

"I'm a kid," Mabel managed to say. "I don't know anything."

"What's wrong with this family?" Jeanne complained. "I ask a simple question that anyone could answer and —"

The front door opened and Violet appeared. She had on her flippers. She was wearing a dress that was way too big for

her and a pointy wizard hat that covered half her face.

"Do *you* know who installed the pool?" Jeanne asked Violet. "No one else around here knows anything."

"I do," Violet said.

"Finally!" Jeanne leaned forward eagerly.

"It was *me*," Violet said.

Mabel shut her eyes tightly and held her breath. There was a very, very long pause.

Then her father started laughing. "Very funny, Violet," he said.

"Violet, you take the cake," her mother said. She leaned over to kiss her on the cheek.

"The pie," Violet corrected. "I take the pie. I *bake* the pie, too."

"It's an expression, silly," Mabel said, secretly relieved that they had changed the subject.

"Is that all you have to say?" Jeanne asked. "Is that your final word?"

"Have you tried the yellow pages?" Mabel's mother asked.

Jeanne shook her head in disgust. "The people who lived here before *always* shared information."

She stomped down the driveway.

"Come on, Violet, let's get the pies ready," Mabel's mother said, before anyone could ask any more questions. She took Violet's hand and led her back into the house.

"Your mother is a mystery to me," Mabel's father said.

"Yes, Dad." Mabel had begun to breathe again.

That was *way* too close for her. She hoped that they would get through the rest of the day without another incident.

Chapter Seventeen

The end-of-summer garage sale was over.

All fourteen families were gathered around a long table laden with pies.

Each pie had a card with a number and name, as in Number Seven, Blueberry Raspberry Delight. That was Mabel's mother's pie. She had also baked Number Two, Lemon Meringue, and Number Eleven, Apple Walnut Cranberry.

One of the neighbors began to cut slices of pie for the judges to taste.

"Which one is yours, Violet?" Simone asked.

Violet pointed to a slightly burned pie at

the back of the table. It was Number Thirteen, Blackberry Surprise.

"Great job," Simone said. "I can't believe you did that all by yourself."

"I couldn't bake a pie when *I* was five," Mabel said. "Not like that."

Looking at its lumps and bumps and blackened spots, she was relieved. That pie was clearly not magical.

"Look at the plum pie," Simone said. "That's my kind. I can't wait to taste it."

"I like Mom's Blueberry Raspberry Delight," Mabel said loyally.

"Number Eleven!" called the judges. They tasted thin slivers of the Apple Walnut Cranberry and wrote down their ratings on the scorecard. "Number Twelve!"

"I wonder if Peter is going to win again this year," someone said. "His grape pie is really to die for."

Mabel said, "I hope Mom wins! Or maybe *you* will, Violet!" She nudged her little sister with her elbow. "You might be the best new pie-maker, or the youngest in contest."

She hoped they had a special category for kindergartners who baked burned pies. Violet deserved an award today.

There hadn't been any magic in the last few hours. There hadn't been any more embarrassing questions. There hadn't been any more fibs or hastily made-up stories.

"We're ready for Number Thirteen," a judge said. "Blackberry Surprise. I love surprises!"

"That's *you*, Violet!" Simone cried.

The pie cutter held a knife over Violet's pie.

"What's he going to do?" Violet whispered in alarm.

"Cut your pie, silly. So the judges can taste it!"

Violet looked nervous. "Will it hurt?"

"Of course not!" Simone patted her on the head.

"I can't wait," Mabel lied. She promised

herself to eat the whole slice, no matter how disgusting it tasted.

Their neighbor picked up a clean knife and sliced into the lumpy crust.

Suddenly there was a sound of singing birds. And then, as the neighbors looked on, four-and-twenty blackbirds flew out of the pie.

They flew over the table, pecking cherries from one of the open pies.

"Surprise!" Violet yelled.

13
BLACKBERRY
SURPRISE

But no one paid attention. People seemed confused, shocked, and stunned.

Violet was jubilant. "I did it! And they didn't get hurt!"

She waved proudly at the birds, who flew around her head in a circle and then disappeared.

The judges had dropped their cards. The neighbors were scratching their heads. Dogs were gobbling bits of crust that the blackbirds had scattered.

"A freak accident," someone said. The words went around the crowd. People shrugged and went back to what they had been doing before.

Was that part of the magic?

Mabel looked around for her parents. They had disappeared. Someone told her that they had gone to get more paper plates and cups.

The judges called out for Pie Number Fourteen, Lemon-Strawberry Meringue.

Mabel let out a long breath. Had she and

Violet gotten away with it *again*? It seemed almost too good to be true.

But then she saw Simone.

Simone was looking at the sky where the blackbirds had disappeared. She turned

to Mabel with a frown. "I'm going to investigate this," she said.

Mabel wanted to crawl under the pie table. But instead, she sat down and took a pen and some paper from her pocket.

It was time to come up with a plan.

About the Author

Anne Mazer is a Mabel who secretly wants to be a Violet. She grew up in a family of writers in upstate New York. She is the author of more than thirty-five books for young readers, including the Scholastic series The Amazing Days of Abby Hayes and the picture book *The Salamander Room*.